Pokémon World

Words and Music by John Loeffler (ASCAP)/John Siegler (BMI)

Rap:

So you wanna be a master of
POKÉMON
Understand the Secrets and
HAVE SOME FUN
So you wanna be a master of Pokémon
POKÉMON
Do you have the skills to be
NUMBER ONE?

Verse I:

I wanna take the ultimate step
Find the courage to be bold
To risk it all and not forget
The lessons that I hold

I wanna go where no one's been
Far beyond the crowd
Learn the way to take command
Use the power that's in my hand

Chorus:

We all live in a Pok
I want to be the gre
We all live in a Pok
Put myself to the te
Be better than all th

Verse II:

Every day along the way
I will be prepared
With every challenge I will gain
Knowledge to be shared

In my heart there's no doubt
Of who I want to be
Right here standing strong
The greatest Master of Pokémon

Chorus:

Rap: You've got the power right in your hands

Copyright © 1999 Jigglypuff Music (ASCAP) / Pikachu Music (BMI)
Rights for Jiggly Puff Music administered by Cherry Lane Music Publishing Company, Inc.
Rights for Pikachu Music administered by Cherry River Music Co. (BMI)
All Rights Reserved   Used by Permission

There are more books about Pokémon.

Collect them all!

coming soon

Tough Enough

Adapted by Tracey West

SCHOLASTIC INC.
New York   Toronto   London   Auckland   Sydney
Mexico City   New Delhi   Hong Kong   Buenos Aires

JOHTO REGION

If you purchased this book without a cover, you should be aware that this book is stolen property. It was reported as "unsold and destroyed" to the publisher, and neither the author nor the publisher has received any payment for this "stripped book."

No part of this book may be reproduced, stored in a retrieval system, or transmitted in any form or by any means, electronic, mechanical, photocopying, recording, or otherwise, without written permission of the publisher. For information regarding permission, write to Scholastic Inc., Attention: Permissions Department, 555 Broadway, New York, NY 10012.

ISBN 0-439-35801-9

© 1995-2001 Nintendo, CREATURES, GAME FREAK.
TM & ® are trademarks of Nintendo.
Copyright © 2001 Nintendo.
All rights reserved. Published by Scholastic Inc.
SCHOLASTIC and associated logos are trademarks
and/or registered trademarks of Scholastic Inc.

12 11 10 9 8 7 6 5   7/0

Printed in the U.S.A.
First Scholastic printing, March 2002

POKÉMON

THE JOHTO JOURNEYS

Tough Enough

The Big Red Pokémon

"What's that noise?" Ash Ketchum asked.

Ash and his friends, Brock and Misty, were walking through a dark forest. Pikachu, Ash's yellow Pokémon, rode on top of Ash's red and white baseball cap.

"I didn't hear anything," said Brock.

Ash shrugged. "Okay," he said. The friends kept walking.

Ash's feet crunched against dry leaves as he walked. Then he heard it again.

Woosh!

"I know I heard something that time!" Ash said.

Misty nodded. Her big blue eyes looked worried. She hugged Togepi, her small spike ball Pokémon, close to her.

"I heard it too," Misty whispered, "and I don't like how it sounded!"

"Check it out, Pikachu," Ash told his Pokémon.

"Pika!" Pikachu said. It jumped off of Ash's head and ran toward the sound.

Woosh! Woosh! Woosh! Ash could see something now. A red blur was whipping through the trees.

Suddenly, a Pokémon leaped out from behind the leaves and stepped in the trail in front of them. The Pokémon was as tall as Brock. It had a shiny red body, two large claws for hands, and insect-like wings on its back.

Pikachu faced the strange Pokémon. Even though Pikachu was much smaller, it didn't back down. Sparks sizzled on its red cheeks.

Ash didn't know what the red Pokémon was up to, but it didn't look friendly. He started to give Pikachu a command.

"Pikachu, use your —"

"Ash, wait!" Brock interrupted him. "That thing is waiting for Pikachu to make the first move," Brock said. "If it's the wrong move, Pikachu could get hurt."

Ash looked at the Pokémon. There was a dangerous gleam in its eye.

Pikachu strained to keep up the electric

charge. Ash knew it was waiting for a command.

"What do you think I should do?" Ash asked. He didn't want to make the wrong move — this Pokémon looked tough.

"I don't know," Brock said. "But if you ask me, it doesn't have a trainer."

"I am its trainer!" a voice boomed.

A tall man stepped out from behind the trees. He had a long, black mustache and wore a black shirt and pants. The red Pokémon broke its attack stance and jumped, landing next to the man.

The whole time, Pikachu was sizzling with electric energy. When the Pokémon jumped away, Pikachu fainted with exhaustion.

"Pikachu!" Ash cried.

2

The Pokémon Training Center

Ash ran to Pikachu's side. "Are you okay?" he asked it. Pikachu was his friend, as well as his top Pokémon. He smiled as Pikachu got back on its feet.

Misty ran up to the trainer. "What's the idea of letting your Pokémon loose?" she asked him. "Don't you know somebody could get hurt?"

The man smiled apologetically. "I'm sorry. My Pokémon and I were doing some secret training," he said. "My name is Muramasa. This is my Scizor, Masamune."

"A Scizor, huh?" Ash said. So that's what the red Pokémon was. Ash pulled out Dexter, his handheld computer, to get more information.

"Scizor, the scissors Pokémon," said the Pokédex. "The evolved form of Scyther. Scizor's incredible attack speed and its large scissorlike claws make it a formidable opponent."

Ash had seen a Scyther before. His friend Tracey had captured one.

"Scizor kind of looks like a bigger, redder Scyther," Ash remarked.

"Yeah, but Scizor's a lot more powerful," Brock said.

Muramasa eyed Ash. "You look like a good trainer," he said. "And I'm impressed with your Pikachu. Why don't you come with me to my elite Pokémon training center?"

Ash wasn't sure what Muramasa had in mind, but he never passed up a chance to see something new. Ever since he had become a Pokémon trainer, he had journeyed through so many different towns and cities. In each place he met lots of new people — and new Pokémon. Sometimes he even caught new Pokémon that he could train. He always learned something wherever he went, and that brought him one step closer to his goal: to become a Pokémon Master.

"What do you say, guys?" Ash asked his friends. "Let's check it out!"

Muramasa led them through the woods to a long, one-story building that sat in the middle of a green field. A Pokémon battle-field, shaped like a rectangle, had been laid out in the brown dirt in front.

As they got closer, Ash saw several trainers and their Pokémon working out. Machoke, a muscled Fighting Pokémon, karate-chopped a block of wood in half. Golem, a combination Rock and Ground Pokémon, lifted a bar of heavy weights above its head. Primeape, a Fighting Pokémon with a round, furry body, was jumping rope. Ash recognized them as some of the toughest Pokémon around.

"Young trainers from all over the world come here to strengthen themselves and their Pokémon," Muramasa said proudly.

"All I ask is that they work diligently to accomplish their dreams of being victorious in their Pokémon battles."

At the sight of Muramasa, each of the trainers gave a small bow. "Good morning, teacher," they said at once.

"I guess the first thing they teach in this school is how to be polite," Misty remarked.

The trainers went back to their routines. Ash and his friends followed some of them inside the center. Brock stopped a boy about Ash's age.

"Your teacher must be a really accomplished Pokémon trainer if so many students come here to learn from him," Brock said.

The boy nodded. "He won a lot of battles in his day," he said. "And his Scizor is awesome, too. It moves so fast they used to call it the Crimson Streak."

"The Crimson Streak. That's pretty cool!" Ash said.

"It used to be!" said a voice.

Ash turned around. The voice belonged to

a boy with purple hair. He wore a red and black striped shirt. He carried a laptop computer under his arm.

Muramasa walked up. He must have heard the boy's comment, but he didn't seem to mind. "This is Shingo, my top student," he said. "Perhaps you could interest him in a Pokémon battle."

Ash never turned down a Pokémon match. "That's fine with me," he said, then turned to Shingo. "I'm Ash Ketchum from Pallet Town. Where are you from?"

Shingo sat down on the ground and opened up his laptop. He started typing furiously.

"Let's see . . . Ketchum . . . Pallet Town," Shingo muttered as he typed.

"Hey, am I in there?" Ash couldn't believe it.

Shingo nodded. "This is my trainer file. It has statistics on noteworthy trainers going back five years. This is everything I need to know about Pokémon and their strategies."

Ash watched as his picture popped up on

the computer screen. There was writing, too, but he wasn't close enough to read it.

Shingo studied the screen. "According to my data, you're a type 'C' trainer," he said. "You use fairly standard attacks and you rely on your Pokémon's power to win for you."

Misty grinned. "He's got *that* right!"

"You make rash decisions and you rely on your hunches," Shingo continued.

Brock nodded. "I'd say that's fairly accurate."

"I see you lost a battle at the Indigo

Plateau because your Charizard wouldn't obey you," Shingo said.

Ash cringed. The information was true, but it didn't tell the whole story. It made him sound like a bad trainer.

"Well, I'm way better now than I was then," Ash said. "Let's battle and I'll show you."

Shingo snapped the laptop shut and stood up.

"Sorry, but my data says you'll lose," said Shingo. "There's no point in battling you."

Ash couldn't believe what he was hearing.

"There's no reason for me to have Pokémon battles anymore," Shingo said. He turned to Muramasa. "If you want me to battle so much, find an opponent who can teach me something I don't already know. Now excuse me." Shingo walked away and up the stairs.

Muramasa apologized for Shingo's behavior and invited Ash and his friends to have a snack. Ash was still steaming as he sipped his hot chocolate.

"Shingo thinks he can learn everything about Pokémon from his computer," Muramasa said. "But he has forgotten the true spirit of Pokémon. He needs someone to challenge him, to make him battle, and get him away from that computer."

Ash stood up. "That does it," he said. "Somebody's got to battle Shingo. And that somebody's going to be me — whether he likes it or not!"

Team Rocket Attacks!

Ash and Pikachu dragged Shingo to the battle area. He protested the whole way as Misty, Brock, and Muramasa watched from the sidelines.

"I told you, Ash," Shingo said, crossly. "You don't have a chance!"

Suddenly, a loud crash followed by a scream drowned out Shingo's complaints.

"What was that?" Ash wondered.

The scream came from the training center. A white Pokémon was lying in the grass, clutching Shingo's laptop computer. A girl with red hair was pulling on the computer cord, trying to reel in the Pokémon. Behind her was a boy with purple hair. The boy and girl wore white uniforms with a red letter "R" emblazoned on the front.

Ash knew the terrible trio. They were Jessie, James, and their Pokémon, Meowth — a notorious team of Pokémon thieves. Usually, they tried to steal his Pikachu.

"Team Rocket!" Ash cried. He started to run toward them, but Muramasa's Scizor was there in a flash. Scizor grabbed the computer cord in one claw and picked up Meowth in the other.

"What are you three doing this time?" Brock demanded.

"We want the data in that computer," said James, the purple-haired boy. "We can use it to steal the best Pokémon in the world!"

Jessie, the red-haired girl, frowned. "Enough chat. Let's battle for it!" she screeched.

Jessie threw two red-and-white Poké Balls. Arbok, a purple cobra Pokémon, flew

out of one. Lickitung, a pink Pokémon with a long tongue, popped out of another.

James threw two Poké Balls, too. Weezing, a purple Pokémon that looked like a cloud of smog with two heads, flew out and belched. Victreebel, a combination Grass and Poison Pokémon, hopped onto the ground. Then it promptly swallowed James inside its big bell-shaped body.

"Here we go again," James mumbled. Then Victreebel spit him out.

Shingo ignored the dangerous-looking Pokémon and ran for his computer. Arbok lunged right at him, baring its long fangs.

"Masamune!" Muramasa called to his Scizor.

Scizor dropped Meowth and dashed in front of Arbok, knocking down the cobra Pokémon. Shingo had grabbed his computer and began typing furiously.

"Team Rocket, eh?" he said. "That's funny. I can't find you guys in here anywhere."

Jessie and James forgot about their attack for a moment.

17

"But we're the world famous Team Rocket," she said. "We must be in your database."

"Your data must be seriously flawed," added James.

Shingo stood up. There was an angry scowl on his face. "I'll show you! My data file is perfect," Shingo said. He threw out a Poké Ball of his own. "Go!"

18

A large red Pokémon popped out. It was another Scizor, just like Muramasa's.

"This is Blade," said Shingo proudly. "It's faster, sharper, stronger, and lasts longer than Muramasa's scizor — and it's never been defeated in battle!"

Shingo knelt down in the dirt, with the computer on his lap. "Get ready, Blade," he said. "After their first attack I'll run a complete analysis on these trainers."

Jessie snickered. "You little dweeb," she said.

"We'll teach you, techno-geek!" James taunted.

"Arbok! Lickitung! Clean out his hard drive!" Jessie yelled.

"Weezing! Victreebel! Tackle Attack!" shouted James.

Meowth bared its sharp claws. "I'll show him my Fury Swipes!"

The five Pokémon began to charge forward.

Shingo smirked. "Reaction speed, point three-four," he said. "To Blade that's like standing still!"

Meowth, Arbok, Lickitung, Weezing, and Victreebel ignored Shingo and continued their charge.

"Use Quick Attack!" Shingo told his Scizor.

Blade began to fly in swift circles around the approaching Pokémon. Soon all Ash could see was a white light as the fast-moving Shingo became a blur.

Then Shingo rammed into Team Rocket's Pokémon. The impact sent the Pokémon flying toward Jessie and James. In a split second, the terrible trio and their Pokémon went soaring into the sky.

"We're blasting off again!" cried Jessie, James, and Meowth.

"Excellent work," said Muramasa.

Shingo shrugged. "I knew I would win. The data predicted it," he said. "So you see, Ash, I don't have to battle you to know that you're going to lose!"

4

Scizor vs. Heracross

"The data predicts everything," Shingo said.

"No it doesn't!" Ash protested. "It doesn't predict how a battle will affect the Pokémon and their trainers. If you competed more, you would know that."

Shingo chuckled. "All right, Ash. I can see you won't give up."

Ash and Shingo took their places on opposite sides of the battlefield. Muramasa stood on the center sideline. He would officiate the match.

"Each trainer will use only one Poké-mon," Muramasa said. "Shingo chooses Blade. Ash chooses . . ."

"I choose Heracross!" Ash said. He threw out a Poké Ball and Heracross popped out. The Bug Pokémon was almost as tall as Ash. Heracross's tough skin was grayish black, and it had a long horn that curved up over its head.

From the sideline, Brock nodded approvingly. "Scizor's strengths are speed and attack power. Ash must be using Heracross because it puts up a great defense."

Shingo shrugged. "That's the obvious choice," he scoffed.

"Begin!" Muramasa yelled.

Shingo typed something into his laptop. Then he looked up. "All right, Blade. Quick Attack!"

Ash countered, "Heracross, give your Leer Attack a try!"

Blade flew across the battlefield, aimed for Heracross. A red light glowed in Heracross's eyes as it got ready for the Leer Attack.

"Blade is flying too fast for the Leer Attack to work!" Brock said.

He was right. Blade slammed into Heracross before the singlehorn Pokémon could attack. Heracross was knocked backward, but its tough skin prevented it from being knocked out.

"At this speed, Blade's Quick Attack delivers three times more damage than normal," Shingo said smugly. "If you had my data you'd know that!"

"We'll see about that," Ash called back. "Heracross, try to get up!"

Heracross got to its feet. It glared at Blade.

"Use your Metal Claw," Shingo told Blade.

Blade grabbed Heracross's horn with its huge claw. Heracross struggled as Blade lifted it into the air.

"Now toss it, Blade!" Shingo yelled.

"Heracross, don't let it throw you!" Ash called out.

Heracross used all its energy to pry itself

out of Blade's claw. It hopped back down to the ground.

"Heracross, use your Horn Attack now!" Ash commanded.

"Dodge it, Blade!" Shingo shouted.

Heracross lowered its horn and slammed right into Blade. The Scizor couldn't get out of the way!

Shingo looked shocked. "Your Heracross couldn't have made that move," he said. "My data says it's not possible."

"That's because Ash battles on instinct," Misty said.

"Different trainers have different styles," Brock added. "That's what makes Pokémon battles so unpredictable!"

Ash knew he had Shingo rattled. For his next command, he chose Take Down. Shingo countered with Agility.

Blade ran superfast circles around Heracross, just as he had done with Team Rocket's Pokémon. Heracross started to sweat.

"Don't try to chase it, Heracross," Ash advised. "Just relax and let Blade come to you."

Heracross closed its eyes. Blade whizzed closer and closer. When Heracross opened its eyes, Blade was no longer a blur. It could focus clearly on the Pokémon's shape.

Blade raised its claw, ready to attack. But Heracross was ready. It rammed into Blade with its powerful horn.

Slam! Blade hit the dirt.

Ash shouted for Heracross to finish the

job. Blade hopped to its feet. The two began to duel: Heracross began to lunge at Blade with its horn, but Blade traded blows using its heavy claws. Soon the two were locked in combat. They looked evenly matched.

Ash held his breath as Blade broke free and flew straight up in the air. Then it dove down, aimed at Heracross's head.

"Stand your ground, Heracross!" Ash yelled.

Heracross ducked its head. Blade's attack landed harmlessly on Heracross's strong back.

Shingo was growing more and more frustrated. He told Blade to repeat the move. Shingo dive-bombed Heracross again.

"Horn Attack!" Ash yelled.

This time, Heracross scooped up Blade in its curved horn. It slammed Blade into the ground.

The slam knocked the wind out of Blade. The Scizor lay sprawled on the ground, motionless.

"Ash wins the match!" Muramasa cried.

5

A Thief on the Loose

Shingo ran to his Pokémon's side.

"Blade, are you okay?" he asked anxiously.

Blade sat up and nodded.

"What about your computer?" Muramasa asked Shingo.

"I don't need it anymore," Shingo replied. "I forgot what real matches were like."

Muramasa smiled and turned to look at his own Scizor. "Shingo's battling spirit has been restored," he said. "And I think ours has, too."

Ash was glad he had helped out Muramasa and Shingo. His Heracross had done a great job against Blade — that Scizor was one tough Pokémon.

"I wonder if we'll face tougher Pokémon than Scizor in the Johto Region." Ash said to his friends the next day. They had shopped for supplies in town, then walked back to the woods and got on the trail that led to their next destination.

"Who knows?' Misty said. "The Johto Region is full of surprises."

Soon they came to a clearing with a picnic table and benches.

"Let's stop and have lunch," Brock suggested.

"Good idea," Ash said. "I'll look for water."

Ash took off his heavy backpack filled with food and supplies. He kept all of his important stuff — his Poké Balls and his Pokédex, in his vest pockets.

It took awhile for him and Pikachu to find water. When Ash returned to the camp, Brock had a fire going. Misty played with Togepi on the picnic table.

"We got the water!" Ash announced.

"Great," Brock said. "Grab the bread and we'll dig in."

Ash walked to the tree where he had stashed his backpack.

It was gone.

"Hey, what happened to my backpack?" Ash asked. He and Pikachu walked around the clearing, checking every tree. The backpack was nowhere in sight.

"Do you think somebody stole it?" Ash wondered.

"We've been here the whole time, and we haven't seen or heard anything," Misty said.

Misty and Brock joined in the search. Suddenly Brock let out a cry.

Ash ran to Brock's side. His friend was pointing to a footprint in the dirt.

A Pokémon footprint.

"I'm not sure what kind of Pokémon it belongs to," Brock said.

"It doesn't matter," said Ash. "Whatever Pokémon left that footprint must have taken my backpack. And I'm going to find it!"

The friends left behind their plans for lunch and followed the footprints. Pikachu led the way.

The prints led out of the woods to the edge of a small town. Ash saw Nurse Joy and her helper, a round, pink Pokémon called Chansey. Every town had a nurse named Joy who worked at the Pokémon Center, healing Pokémon and giving them a good meal.

Nurse Joy and Chansey were looking into a grocery bag and frowning.

"Is everything okay?" Ash asked.

"I put the bag down for a minute and now a ham is missing," she said. "It's very strange."

Ash told her about his missing backpack with the bread inside.

"Oh my!" said Nurse Joy.

"Pika! Pika!" Pikachu was excited about something at the side of the road.

The Pokémon had discovered another set of footprints that matched the first. These led back into the forest, but in a new direction.

"We'd better hurry up and catch it before it gets away," Ash said. "Let's go!"

Night of the Houndour

They followed the footprints as far as they could, but the trail disappeared in the middle of the woods.

"Don't worry, Ash," Brock said. "I have an idea."

They made their way back to the clearing and Brock started another fire. Then he put a pot of hot dogs over the flames to boil. While the fire blazed, Brock began to carve something from a piece of tree branch as he explained his plan.

"The wind will carry the smell of the food," Brock said.

"I get it," Ash said. "The Pokémon that stole our stuff will try to get it, right?"

"Right," Brock said, nodding. He held up the piece of wood he was whittling. It was shaped like a hot dog. "But instead, it'll get this meaty little decoy."

Misty shivered. "I hope it doesn't get us," she said.

Ash understood Misty's fear. The sun had set, and the woods looked dark and spooky. Who knows what kind of Pokémon was lurking out there?

The friends took the hot dogs out of the pot and left the decoy in place. They hid behind some bushes to watch the campsite.

Suddenly, the fire went out. Ash heard a rustling noise. Pikachu's ears twitched.

Ash turned away from the camp. "What's out there, Pikachu?" he asked.

There was another rustling noise. Ash turned back around.

"The bait is gone!" Ash cried.

"Whatever took it got away again," Misty said.

Brock didn't seem worried. "That went perfectly," he said. "The thief took the fake food. If it wants the real deal, it will have to come back again."

Ash was impressed. Brock's plan was really smart. When the Pokémon came back, he'd be ready for it this time.

They didn't have long to wait. A low, growling sound filled the night. A chill traveled down Ash's spine.

The friends stepped into the clearing. The growling sound seemed to be all around them. Togepi shivered in Misty's arms. Pikachu scanned the surrounding trees.

Then Ash saw a pair of red eyes peering out of the darkness.

And another. And another. And another.

They were dealing with four Pokémon, not one.

"What are you waiting for?" Ash challenged them. "Come on out!"

Four black Pokémon slinked out of the

37

trees. The Pokémon walked on all fours. Each one had a sleek, muscled body and an angry-looking snout.

"Guess we'd better check these guys out," Ash said. He took out his Pokédex.

"Houndour, the dark Pokémon," Dexter said. "Houndour travel in packs and communicate through barks in order to surround their prey."

One of the Pokémon stepped forward. It dropped the fake hot dog on the ground and growled.

"I guess it didn't enjoy your little trick," Misty said.

"Maybe that wasn't such a good idea," Brock admitted.

Misty's voice rose to an angry pitch. "Maybe you should have thought of that before!" she yelled.

Grrrrrrrr.

Something else was growling now. Ash looked in the direction of the noise.

A fifth Houndour was standing on top of a tall rock.

"That must be the leader of the pack," Brock remarked.

"I don't care who you are," Ash told the Houndour. "I want my backpack back!"

The lead Houndour leaped off of the rock. It stood with the other Houndour. The five Pokémon growled menacingly.

"I think they're going to attack!" Misty cried.

7

A Friend in Need

"Fine," said Ash. "We'll do this the hard way."

Ash took two Poké Balls out of his vest and threw them in the air.

"Go, Cyndaquil! Go, Chikorita!" he yelled.

The two Pokémon burst onto the scene. Cyndquil, a Fire Pokémon, had a sleek body and a long snout. Chikorita, a Grass Pokémon, had a light green body. Two dark green leaves grew on top of its smooth head.

Misty and Brock threw Poké Balls, too. Brock called on Onix, a huge Rock Pokémon that looked like a long serpent made of boulders. Misty tried to call on her Staryu, but Psyduck popped out instead. The Water Pokémon had orange feathers, a wide bill, and a confused look on its face.

Pikachu, Cyndaquil, Chikorita, Onix, and Psyduck lined up in front of the Houndour.

"Five on five," Ash said. "At least we're not outnumbered."

The Houndour didn't let the trainers make the first move. They charged at the Pokémon.

One Houndour leaped at Cyndaquil, baring its white fangs. Cyndaquil dodged out of the way just in time.

Another Houndour leaped at Psyduck. The poor Pokémon didn't have time to muster up a Confusion Attack. Luckily, Chikorita used Razor Leaf to knock the Houndour out of the way. Sharp leaves shot out of Chikorita's body, pounding the attacking Pokémon.

At the same time, a Houndour jumped up behind Ash. Luckily, Brock saw it. He sent

Onix after it. Onix dove after the Houndour, crash-landing in the dirt. Two Houndour jumped on Onix's back.

"Pikachu, use your Thundershock now!" Ash cried.

Pikachu quickly obeyed. Sizzling bolts of lightning jumped from Pikachu's body and zapped the two Houndour. They jumped off of Onix, yelping loudly.

The sound of its fallen pack members made the lead Houndour angry. It jumped in front of Pikachu. The other four Houndour stepped aside.

"It looks like the Houndour leader wants to have a one-on-one battle with Ash," Brock said.

"If it wants a battle we'll give it one. Right, Pikachu?" Ash said confidently.

Pikachu nodded, never taking its eyes off of the lead Houndour. Its eyes began to glow an eerie red color.

"Careful, Ash," Brock said. "Houndour is using its Leer Attack!"

Misty looked worried. "It looks pretty powerful. Do you think Pikachu can take it?"

"Of *course* Pikachu can take it," Ash snapped back. "Use your Leer Attack right back at Houndour!"

Pikachu started its Leer Attack, but the Houndour changed its strategy. Ferocious flames burst from its mouth. Pikachu jumped out of the way, countering with a powerful electric shock.

The Houndour had quick reflexes, too. It deflected the shock with its short, powerful tail.

The exchange took a lot out of both Pokémon. They faced each other, panting heavily.

The other four Houndour flanked their leader.

Thick, black smoke poured from the mouths of all five Houndour. The foul-smelling smoke filled the clearing. Ash choked and his eyes teared up. He couldn't see anything thanks to the Smog Attack.

When the smog cleared, Ash saw the Houndour disappearing into the woods.

"Let's follow them!" he cried. "I won't stop until I get my backpack."

Misty and Brock groaned, but they followed anyway. This time, they didn't lose the trail. They followed the Houndour to a cave cut into the bottom of a hill.

Ash wasn't prepared to see a sixth Houndour in front of the cave. It looked sick. Ash saw his backpack and a half-eaten ham near the cave.

But that wasn't all. A Golem was attacking the sick Houndour. The massive Pokémon had a round body made of heavy rocks. It stood on two small, sturdy legs, and long claws extended from its gray hands.

One by one, the Houndour pack jumped down to the cave and lunged at the Golem. The lead Houndour aimed a shower of flame at the Golem. The big gray Pokémon tucked in its head, legs, and arms into a ball. It rolled across the dirt, slamming into the lead Houndour.

The impact sent the Houndour sprawling. But Golem wasn't finished. It came rolling at the lead Houndour again. The Houndour got ready to blast the Golem with another flame.

Ash knew it was pointless. The fire attacks

wouldn't work against Golem, a combination Rock and Ground Pokémon. There was only one thing to do.

Ash threw his body between the lead Houndour and the Golem. He dragged the Houndour away just in time. The Golem got ready for another attack.

"Chikorita, Razor Leaf!" Ash yelled.

Sharp green leaves zipped through the air and hit the Golem. They were moving so fast that they sent the Golem rolling away, far from the cave.

Brock hurried to the side of the sick Houndour. The Pokémon was lying on its side and breathing heavily.

Brock gently examined it. Then he looked up.

"Its leg is hurt, and it's burning up with fever," Brock said.

Ash turned to the lead Houndour. "Your friend here is in really bad shape," he said, hoping it would understand. "We have to get it to the Pokémon Center fast!"

8

A Houndour Heist

The lead Houndour stared at Ash for a few seconds, sizing him up. Then the dark Pokémon turned to another and nodded.

Ash knew that meant that they could help the injured Houndour. He bent down and hoisted the Houndour onto his back.

"You wait here," he told the other Houndour. "I'll be back before you know it."

"Hold it, twerp!" cried a shrill voice.

The voice belonged to Jessie of Team Rocket. Jessie, James, and Meowth were standing on top of a rock overlooking the cave.

"Leave us alone," Ash said, sounding more annoyed than threatened. "We're in the middle of something very important."

Jessie laughed. "You're not going anywhere until we get Pikachu, those Houndour, and the ham they stole from us!"

"So you took the ham from Nurse Joy, and the Houndour stole it from you!" Misty said.

"Well, sort of," Jessie admitted sheepishly.

"We usually just steal Pokémon," James added, "but we were hungry!"

"Keep the ham," Meowth said. "We'll take Pikachu and the Houndour."

The Houndour leader ran between Ash and Team Rocket. The Pokémon barked something to Ash.

Meowth translated the Houndour's speech. "It said, you kids go on ahead. We'll take care of these three jokers!"

Ash hated to leave Houndour fighting Team Rocket on their own. But the sick Houndour needed help — and fast. He nodded back to the lead Houndour.

"We'll be back as soon as we can," he said.

Ash, Misty, Brock, and Pikachu hurried away from the cave as fast as they could. Ash heard the Houndour growl behind them.

"Don't worry, Ash," Brock said. "Those Houndour are tough. They can handle Team Rocket."

Ash hoped Brock was right. As he ran through the forest, Ash's main concern was the injured Houndour on his back. It needed help.

The friends ran and ran. Ash's burden seemed to grow heavier and heavier. Then he lost his footing. Ash slipped and fell, but didn't lose hold of the Houndour.

Brock helped him up. "Let me carry it now," he offered.

"No, I can do it," Ash said stubbornly. He rose to his feet, but his knees buckled under again.

Suddenly, a pair of red eyes appeared in the darkness. It was the lead Houndour! The rest of the pack stood behind it.

"They must have taken care of Team Rocket," Misty said, relieved.

The Houndour barked something, nodding at the sick Houndour. Ash understood.

"Okay. You can carry your friend," he said. "We're almost there."

They didn't have far to go. They burst through the doors of the Pokémon Center and called to Nurse Joy. She rushed the poor Pokémon into the examination room.

Ash and the others spent a few fitful hours waiting for word about the sick Pokémon. The lead Houndour waited inside the

Pokémon Center while the other four paced nervously outside. As the morning sun rose, Nurse Joy emerged with a smile on her face.

"Houndour's going to be just fine," she said.

The lead Houndour gave a happy howl.

But their good mood didn't last long. The other four Houndour howled outside — but their howls weren't happy.

Ash and the others rushed outside. A white balloon with a Meowth face floated above the Pokémon Center. Jessie, James, and Meowth stood in the balloon basket. A net dangled over the basket's edge — and inside the net were the four Houndour!

"You didn't think we'd give up that easily, did you, twerps?" Jessie asked.

"It's payback time for busting up our ham scam!" Meowth said.

The balloon rose higher. Team Rocket and the trapped Houndour sailed away from the Pokémon Center.

Ash knew a powerful shock from Pikachu could stop them. But they were too far away!

Then Ash had an idea.

"Houndour, let Pikachu climb on and then jump as high as you can," he told the lead Houndour.

The Pokémon nodded. Pikachu jumped on its back. Houndour charged after the balloon with super speed. Then it leaped in the air, almost as if it had wings.

"Houndour, use your Flamethrower to cut that rope!" Ash cried.

A blast of flame shot out of Houndour's mouth and seared the rope that attached the net to the balloon. The net fell to the ground. The captured Houndour were free!

"Pikachu, jump and finish them off with a Thunderbolt Attack!" Ash called out.

Pikachu jumped straight up in the air, aiming a jagged bolt of lightning at Team Rocket's balloon.

The attack was right on the mark. Team Rocket glowed fluorescent yellow as the electric charge zapped them. The balloon spiraled off into the sky.

"We're blasting off again!" they screamed.

9

The Off-Colored Noctowl

The Houndour leader ran over to Ash and licked his face.

"Hey, that tickles!" Ash said, giggling.

Misty grinned. "It's better to take a licking from a Houndour than from Team Rocket," she joked.

Brock treated all the Houndour to some of his special Pokémon food. Then Ash waved good-bye as all six Houndour returned to their home in the woods.

"Bye, Houndour," Ash called out. "See you all again some day!"

Ash thanked Nurse Joy, and soon he and his friends were on the road again.

"First Scizor, now Houndour," Ash remarked. "I'm pretty impressed with the Pokémon in the Johto Region."

"I know what you mean," Misty said. "Those Houndour did everything they could to help their friend. They never gave up."

Soon, the friends came upon another forest, even darker and spookier than the Houndour forest. It was only noon, but as they walked under the thick trees, it seemed like midnight.

As usual, Pikachu was perched on top of Ash's baseball cap.

"Pika!" said Pikachu. The Pokémon pointed to one of the trees.

"What is it, Pikachu?" Ash asked.

Ash peered into the branches. A tiny house with a round hole for a door was nestled in the crook of the tree.

"I'll bet that belongs to some Flying Pokémon," Misty guessed.

"You're right," Brock said. "But it's too

big for a Pidgey, and too small for a Pidgeot. I wonder what kind of Pokémon lives there?"

Suddenly, a rustling of wings interrupted them. A Flying Pokémon landed on the branch outside of the house. The Pokémon had brown feathers, black wings and markings, a short beak, and a ridge of feathers that rose up over its eyes.

Ash took out Dexter, his pocket Pokédex, and punched buttons until a picture of the Pokémon appeared.

"Noctowl, the Owl Pokémon, is the evolved form of Hoothoot," Dexter said. "Highly intelligent, it often twists its head one hundred and eighty degrees to think more clearly."

"Wow," Brock said. "But Noctowl should only come out at night. This is rare."

"This is a pretty dark forest," Misty pointed out. "Noon and night are pretty much the same thing."

Ash watched to see one if the Noctowl would enter the house.

One of the tree branches started moving strangely. Ash thought he heard a whisper.

The Noctowl flew away.

"Did that tree branch just shoo off that Noctowl?" Ash wondered.

"That's what it looked like," Misty agreed.

Before they could investigate, a smaller Noctowl flew onto the branch. This one had red wings and a red tail instead of black like the larger Pokémon.

The branch moved again. The red Noctowl twisted its head from side to side. Then it reached out with one of its feet and kicked the tree branch.

Ash gasped. A man in a blue suit and eyeglasses was hiding on the tree branch! He started to fall, but managed to grab another branch with one hand.

The Noctowl hopped over to the man's hand. It picked at the man's fingers with its sharp beak.

"Hey!" the man protested.

Then he tumbled to the ground.

10

HYPNOSIS!

Ash ran up to the fallen man. "Are you okay, sir?" he asked.

The man stood up and smoothed out his gray shirt. He adjusted his eyeglasses. "I was trying to catch that off-colored Noctowl, but I failed again," he said, scowling a little. "My name is Dr. Wiseman. I collect rare Pokémon."

"I'd love to catch one myself," Ash said.

Dr. Wiseman raised an eyebrow. "You? There's no way. That one is much smarter than your average Noctowl. Chances to

catch one of these Pokémon don't come along very often."

That sounded like just the kind of challenge Ash thrived on. Dr. Wiseman kept talking, but Ash was focused on the Noctowl in the tree. He couldn't resist.

"If this one is so great, I've got to catch it," Ash said. He took an empty Poké Ball out of his vest pocket. "Gotta catch that Noctowl!"

Ash missed the shocked look on Dr. Wiseman's face as he hurled the Poké Ball toward the tree. Noctowl did not take its eyes off of the Poké Ball. As the ball approached, Noctowl knocked it back with its foot. The Poké Ball flew through the air bumping Ash in the head!

"Ouch!" Ash complained, rubbing his head.

Noctowl flapped its wings and let out a hoot that sounded a lot like a laugh.

"That thing's making fun of me," Ash said angrily.

Dr. Wiseman smiled smugly. "I told you it wouldn't be easy," he said.

Ash wasn't about to give up. "Pikachu, catch that Noctowl!" Ash cried.

As Ash spoke, glowing red circles appeared in Noctowl's eyes. The red beams floated through the air and landed on Ash's face.

Ash noticed them for a second. Then he forgot about them. A strange feeling latched onto his brain. All he could think about was Pikachu.

But Pikachu didn't seem to be moving. It was like it had ignored Ash's commands. This wasn't like Pikachu at all.

Ash knelt in front of Pikachu and grabbed the Pokémon by the shoulders.

"Come on, Pikachu! Move!" he pleaded. But Pikachu wouldn't budge.

Ash tried to pick Pikachu up. For some reason, Pikachu was much too heavy. Ash fell back onto the ground.

Suddenly, the strange feeling disappeared. Ash looked down. He wasn't grabbing Pikachu at all — he was grabbing a rock! Pikachu was standing a few feet away, looking perplexed.

"What happened?" he asked his friends. Misty was trying to hide a giggle.

"Noctowl used Hypnosis on you, Ash," Dr. Wiseman said. "It made you think that rock was Pikachu."

In the tree above, Noctowl laughed again. Then it flew away.

"I really wanted to catch that Noctowl!" Ash said, disappointed.

Dr. Wiseman invited them back to his cabin for a snack. As they munched on cookies, he told them about his quest to capture the strange-colored Noctowl.

"That Noctowl has been tricking me ever since I met it," he explained. "But it won't make a fool of me any longer. I'll show it how clever I can be!"

"I know how you feel," Ash said. "I just met it, and I want to show it up, too — by catching it."

Dr. Wiseman just shook his head. "You couldn't catch it in a hundred years."

"Well, you haven't caught it either," Ash pointed out.

Dr. Wiseman stood up and walked to the corner of the room. A green cloth covered something big and bulky.

"When my trap is completed, I will catch that Noctowl once and for all," Dr. Wiseman said.

Misty frowned. "A real Pokémon trainer would battle Noctowl fair and square."

"Yeah," Ash agreed. "Just like I'm going to do."

"That's what you think," Dr. Wiseman said. "But my trap is the only way."

A lightbulb went off in Ash's head. "Why don't we compete to see who catches it first?"

Dr. Wiseman shook Ash's hand. "Just what I was thinking. Let the challenge begin!"

Dr. Wiseman worked to put the finishing touches on his trap. In a few hours, he was ready to test it out. Ash let Dr. Wiseman try first.

Back in the woods, they went to the tree where the Noctowl lived. Dr. Wiseman set up his trap. Then he joined Ash, Misty, Brock, Pikachu, and Togepi behind some bushes.

They waited in silence. A few minutes later, the Noctowl with the red wings and markings flew onto the tree branch.

Dr. Wiseman grinned. Then he reached over and began pulling on a rope. Ash saw that the rope went though a series of pulleys. The far end of the rope was attached to some fake tree branches Dr. Wiseman had planted near Noctowl.

As Dr. Wiseman pulled the rope, the tree branches spread apart to reveal a mirror. Noctowl looked in the mirror — and thought it was looking at another Noctowl! Its eyes glowed red as it used Hypnosis against the Noctowl in the mirror.

"Just as I planned," Dr. Wiseman said, smiling.

Noctowl's Hypnosis waves hit the mirror, then reflected right back at Noctowl! The poor Pokémon hypnotized itself.

"I see," said Brock. "Instead of Hypnotizing its opponent, the attack was reflected back onto Noctowl."

Dr. Wiseman laughed. "I've done it! It's a

Pokémon, after all. It can't compete with human intelligence."

Ash felt a little weird about Dr. Wiseman's tactic. It just didn't seem fair.

Noctowl started to teeter back and forth on the branch, as though it were sleepy. Then it fell to the ground.

Dr. Wiseman ran over to it. "I did it! I did it! I caught a Noctowl!" Dr. Wiseman said gleefully.

Ash's heart sank. Had he really lost the Noctowl challenge?

11

Giant Robot Noctowl!

"I caught it! I caught it!" Dr. Wiseman sang as he danced around the Noctowl.

Ash thought Dr. Wiseman was acting kind of strange. Then Dr. Wiseman bent down and started to pick up a rock.

"Boy, this Noctowl is really heavy," Dr. Wiseman said.

"He must have been hypnotized by the Noctowl when he went to capture it," Brock said.

"Where is Noctowl?" Ash wondered. While

Ash was watching Dr. Wiseman, Noctowl had disappeared.

Misty pointed into the woods. "There it is!"

Noctowl was wobbling around, still confused by the Hypnosis Attack.

Ash rushed up behind it. Noctowl turned around and gave an angry cry.

"Be careful, Ash," Brock warned. "It must feel threatened."

Before Ash could plan his next move, a strong wind swept through the forest. It almost blew the cap off of his head.

The wind snapped Dr. Wiseman out of his Hypnosis. "What's going on?" he asked.

The wind grew stronger, and something big came crashing through the trees.

"Prepare for trouble!" shrieked a voice.

"Make it double!" added another.

Ash looked up. The voices belonged to Jessie and James of Team Rocket. They were talking through microphones and piloting a giant robot shaped like a Noctowl. Team Rocket had tied a red balloon to each side of the robot's head to float the robot into the forest. The strong wind was caused by air escaping from the balloons as the robot landed.

"We'll take the Noctowl as a nice little present for our Boss," Meowth said, from his position at the control panel.

Dr. Wiseman seemed impressed. "You mean you built this huge machine to catch one little Pokémon? I like it!"

"We put our all into catching any Pokémon, no matter how small," James said

proudly. "That's the Team Rocket philosophy."

"You should use your Pokémon to battle fair and square," said Brock. "That's the philosophy of a real Pokémon trainer."

Meowth grinned. "Make no mistake. We're not Pokémon trainers. We're Team Rocket! And now we'll catch that Noctowl." The talking Pokémon reached for a lever on the control panel.

"Not so fast!" Ash cried. "Pikachu, Thunderbolt!"

Pikachu obeyed right away. It hurled a powerful bolt of sizzling electricity at the robot.

But the bolt hit the robot's metal surface and bounced right back into the ground.

"The body of this machine is covered with a special coating," James said. "Pikachu's electric attacks won't work!"

Ash was getting angry now. He threw out two more Poké Balls.

"Go Cyndaquil! Go Totodile!" he yelled. The Pokémon burst onto the scene in a blaze of light.

But before he could use his Fire Pokémon and Water Pokémon, Meowth began pressing buttons. The two red balloons inflated quickly. Then he pressed another button, and the balloons deflated again. The wind knocked Cyndaquil and Totodile off of their feet. The Noctowl went flying backward, too. It looked hurt.

In the confusion, Dr. Wiseman grabbed Noctowl in his arms and started to run away.

"Hey, that's not fair!" Ash cried.

"He thinks he can beat Team Rocket?" James was shocked. "We'll show him!"

Meowth hit some more buttons, and two metal legs extended from the bottom of the Noctowl robot. Each leg had a sharp set of metal claws on the end.

Ash watched, helpless, as one claw grabbed Dr. Wiseman by the back of his jacket. Dr. Wiseman lost his grip on Noctowl, but the Pokémon was quickly grabbed by the other metal claw. Then the robot begin to lift off.

Ash thought fast. He threw out another Poké Ball and Bulbasaur popped out. The blue-green Grass Pokémon had a large plant bulb on top of its back.

"Bulbasaur! Chikorita! Use Vine Whip to stop the robot!" Ash yelled.

Thick green vines launched from the two Pokémon. They wrapped around the giant robot, keeping it from flying away.

"I'll help you, Noctowl!" Ash cried. He climbed up a tree. When he was at the same height as the claw that held Noctowl, he leaped off.

Wham! Ash landed on the shiny metal claw. Noctowl was struggling to escape. Ash tried to pry the metal apart. It wasn't easy. The claw was tightly clamped.

"You can't do it, twerp," Jessie taunted him.

"Don't waste your strength, kid," said Meowth. "Give up!"

Team Rocket's comments only made Ash try harder. He pried at the claw with all his might. Noctowl struggled to find an opening.

Then, finally, Ash managed to squeeze open the claw just enough for Noctowl to escape. The Pokémon flew out and landed in a tree next to Ash's Pokémon.

Meowth scowled. "I'll show him!" it cried. It pressed a lever, and the claw moved, sending Ash flying into a clump of bushes.

Ash had the wind knocked out of him, but he was fine. When he stood up, he saw Noctowl screeching something to Cyndaquil, Totodile, and Pikachu.

Cyndaquil nodded and ran up to the robot. It shot a burning stream of fire at the metal monster.

"I think Cyndaquil is following Noctowl's plan," Brock remarked, amazed.

Up in the control booth, Team Rocket just chuckled. "We can take all the fire you can give us," Jessie said confidently.

Noctowl's head twisted from side to side. Then it hooted at Totodile.

Cyndaquil stepped aside, and Totodile squirted the hot metal with a powerful stream of cold water. Ash was starting to get Noctowl's plan.

"Our special metal coating is cracking!" Meowth shrieked.

"Now I see," said Brock. "Spraying cold water on heated metal . . ."

"Will make it crack, no matter how special it is," Misty said.

They were right. A huge seam cracked open in the middle of the robot. The machine's inner workings were exposed.

Ash knew just what to do to finish the job.

"Pikachu, aim a Thunderbolt at that crack!" he cried.

Noctowl's challenge

"Pika!" Pika aimed an even stronger jolt of electricity than before. The jagged bolt was right on target. It sizzled right through the cracked seam.

The Thunderbolt Attack fried the giant robot. The blast sent Team Rocket and their metal machine hurling away.

"Looks like Team Rocket's blasting off again!" they screamed.

Ash thanked his Pokémon for their good work. Then he turned to Noctowl. Was the Pokémon all right?

Noctowl flapped its wings and flew down to a branch on face level with Ash. Then it began to hoot.

"I think Noctowl is trying to say something," Brock said.

Dr. Wiseman listened to the hoots. Then a look of surprise crossed his face.

"Noctowl is challenging you, Ash!" he said.

"Me?" Ash said.

"I've been studying it long enough to know what it wants. I'm disappointed, but I'm not going to stop you," Dr. Wiseman said. "Good luck catching it!"

Ash couldn't believe his luck. He knew just what Pokémon to choose.

"Pikachu," Ash said. "It's up to you. Use Thunderbolt!"

After shocking Team Rocket, Pikachu needed to built up another electric charge. Sparks sizzled on its round, red cheeks. As Pikachu built up energy, Noctowl launched another Hypnosis Attack.

The Hypnosis took effect right away. Pikachu began to wobble around. It tried to aim electric attacks at Noctowl, but it kept missing. Finally, Pikachu shocked itself! The little Pokémon fell backward.

"Pikachu, are you okay?" Ash asked.

Pikachu stood right back up. It seemed like it was back to normal.

"All right!" Ash said. "When it shocked itself, it knocked out the Hypnosis."

Noctowl hooted and flew circles around Pikachu. Then it swooped down out of the sky.

Pikachu ran away as fast as it could.

"Don't look in Noctowl's eyes," Ash called to Pikachu. "Aim your attack at the sound of its beating wings."

Pikachu stopped and closed its eyes. Ash saw its pointy ears twitch as it focused on the sound. Noctowl flew smaller and smaller circles around Pikachu, waiting for the right moment to launch another attack.

Then Pikachu struck. One short, powerful blast of energy zapped Noctowl. It came too quickly for Noctowl to dodge it.

The electric charge sent Noctowl plummeting to the ground. Ash quickly threw an

82

empty Poké Ball at it. The red-and-white ball opened up in midair. A red beam shot out, and Noctowl disapeared inside.

The Poké Ball dropped to the ground. It wiggled for a few seconds. Then it stopped.

Ash ran and picked up the Poké Ball. "I did it!" he cried. "I caught a Noctowl!"

"Nice job, Ash!" Misty cheered.

"Congratulations," Dr. Wiseman said. "That was a beautiful match."

Ash stared at the Poké Ball in his hands. "Catching Noctowl was a real challenge," he said. "It's one smart Pokémon."

"And tough, too," said Misty. "Just like Houndour and Scizor."

"That's right," Brock said. "We've met some pretty powerful Pokémon in the Johto Region."

"Well then this is the perfect place for me," Ash said.

"Oh yeah?" Misty asked. "Why is that?"

Ash grinned. "Because I am one tough trainer!"

POKÉMON

GOTTA READ 'EM ALL!

❏ BDW 0-439-10464-5 **Pokémon Chapter Book #1: I Choose You!** $4.50 US

❏ BDW 0-439-10466-1 **Pokémon Chapter Book #2: Island of the Giant Pokémon** $4.50 US

❏ BDW 0-439-13550-8 **Pokémon Chapter Book #3: Attack of the Prehistoric Pokémon** $4.50 US

❏ BDW 0-439-13742-X **Pokémon Chapter Book #4: Night in the Haunted Tower** $4.50 US

❏ BDW 0-439-15418-9 **Pokémon Chapter Book #5: Team Rocket Blasts Off!** $4.50 US

❏ BDW 0-439-15421-9 **Pokémon Chapter Book #6: Charizard, Go!** $4.50 US

❏ BDW 0-439-15426-X **Pokémon Chapter Book #7: Splashdown in Cerulean City** $4.50 US

❏ BDW 0-439-15429-4 **Pokémon Chapter Book #8: Return of the Squirtle Squad** $4.50 US

❏ BDW 0-439-16942-9 **Pokémon Chapter Book #9: Journey to the Orange Islands** $4.50 US

❏ BDW 0-439-16943-7 **Pokémon Chapter Book #10: Secret of the Pink Pokémon** $4.50 US

❏ BDW 0-439-16944-5 **Pokémon Chapter Book #11: The Four Star Challenge** $4.50 US

❏ BDW 0-439-16945-3 **Pokémon Chapter Book #12: Scyther, Heart of a Champion** $4.50 US

❏ BDW 0-439-20089-X **Pokémon Chapter Book #13: Race to Danger** $4.50 US

❏ BDW 0-439-20090-3 **Pokémon Chapter Book #14: Talent Showdown** $4.50 US

❏ BDW 0-439-20091-1 **Pokémon Chapter Book #15: Psyduck Ducks Out** $4.50 US

❏ BDW 0-439-20092-X **Pokémon Chapter Book #16: Thundershock in Pummelo Stadium** $4.50 US

❏ BDW 0-439-20093-8 **Pokémon Chapter Book #17: Go West, Young Ash** $4.50 US

❏ BDW 0-439-20094-6 **Pokémon Chapter Book #18: Ash Ketchum, Pokémon Detective** $4.50 US

❏ BDW 0-439-22033-5 **Pokémon Chapter Book #19: Prepare for Trouble** $4.50 US

❏ BDW 0-439-24397-1 **Pokemon Chapter Book #20: Battle for the Zephyr Badge** $4.50 US

❏ BDW 0-439-22113-7 **Pokemon Chapter Book #21: The Chikorita Challenge** $4.50 US

❏ BDW 0-439-22114-5 **Pokemon Chapter Book #22: All Fired Up** $4.50 US

❏ BDW 0-439-22092-0 **Pokemon Chapter Book #23: Ash to the Rescue** $4.50 US

❏ BDW 0-439-22091-2 **Pokemon Chapter Book #24: Secrets of the GS Ball** $4.50 US

❏ BDW 0-439-15405-7 **Pokémon Jr. Chapter Book #1: Surf's Up, Pikachu** $3.99 US

❏ BDW 0-439-15417-0 **Pokémon Jr. Chapter Book #2: Meowth, the Big Mouth** $3.99 US

❏ BDW 0-439-15420-0 **Pokémon Jr. Chapter Book #3: Save Our Squirtle!** $3.99 US

❏ BDW 0-439-15427-8 **Pokémon Jr. Chapter Book #4: Bulbasaur's Bad Day** $3.99 US

POKéMON

GOTTA READ 'EM ALL!™

❑ BDW 0-439-15431-6 **Pokémon Jr. Chapter Book #5:** **Two of a Kind** $3.99 US	❑ BDW 0-439-19969-7 **Pokémon Jr. Movie Novelization:** **Pikachu's Rescue Adventure** $4.50 US
❑ BDW 0-439-20095-4 **Pokémon Jr. Chapter Book #6:** **Raichu Shows Off** $3.99 US	❑ BDW 0-439-29488-6 **Pokémon Movie Tie-In Novelization:** **Lord of the Unknown Tower** $4.99 US
❑ BDW 0-439-20096-2 **Pokémon Jr. Chapter Book #7:** **Nidoran's New Friend** $3.99 US	❑ BDW 0-439-10659-1 **The Official** **Pokémon Collector's** **Sticker Book** $5.99 US
❑ BDW 0-439-20097-0 **Pokémon Jr. Chapter Book #8:** **A Pokémon Snow-Down (Dec)** $3.99 US	❑ BDW 0-439-10397-5 **The Official Pokémon** **Handbook** $9.99 US
❑ BDW 0-439-20098-9 **Pokémon Jr. Chapter Book #9:** **Snorlax Takes A Stand (Feb)** $3.99 US	❑ BDW 0-439-1 04-9 **The Official Pokémon** **Handbook: Deluxe Edition** $12.99 US
❑ BDW 0-439-23399-2 **Pokémon Jr. Chapter Book #10:** **Good-bye, Lapras** $3.99 US	❑ BDW 0-439-15424-3 **The Official Collector's** **Sticker Book #2** $5.99 US
❑ BDW 0-439-23400-X **Pokémon Jr. Chapter Book #11:** **Bellossom's Big Battle** $3.99 US	❑ BDW 0-439-15406-5 **Pokémon Pop Quiz!** **A Total Trivia and** **Test Your Knowledge Book!** $3.99 US
❑ BDW 0-439-13741-1 **Pokémon Movie Tie-In Novelization:** **Mewtwo Strikes Back** $3.99 US	❑ BDW 0-439-19968-9 **Pokémon: The Power of One** **(2nd Movie Novelization)** $4.99 US
❑ BDW 0-439-29487-8 **Pokémon Jr. Movie Novelization:** **Pikachu and Pichu in the City** $4.50 US	❑ BDW 0-439-19401-6 **Extreme Pokémon** $9.99 US
❑ BDW 0-439-15986-5 **Pokémon Jr. Movie Novelization:** **Pikachu's Vacation** $4.50 US	

Available wherever you buy books, or use this order form.

Scholastic Inc., P.O. Box 7502, Jefferson City, MO 65102

ease send me the books I have checked above. I am enclosing $_____ (please add $2.00 to cover shipping and handling).
nd check or money order — no cash or C.O.D.s please.

Name _____

Address _____

City _____ State/Zip _____

ease allow four to six weeks for delivery. Offer good in the U.S. only. Sorry, mail orders are not available to residents of Canada. Prices
bject to change.

w w w . s c h o l a s t i c . c o m

© 1995-2001 Nintendo, CREATURES, GAME FREAK. TM & ® are trademarks of Nintendo. © 2001 Nintendo.

POK901